For my family and in loving memory of the women who came before us —J. W.

For Elizabeth Riley, who was and always will be my second mother —H. T.

SHOW WAY
JACQUELINE WOODSON
illustrated by HUDSON TALBOTT
G. P. PUTNAM'S SONS

When Soonie's great-grandma was seven, she was sold from the Virginia land to a plantation in South Carolina without her ma or pa but with some muslin her ma had given her.

And two needles she got from the big house— and thread dyed bright red with berries from the chokecherry tree.

In South Carolina, Big Mama raised Soonie's great-grandma.
Raised most the slave children on that large patch of land.

At night, Big Mama told the children stories.
Stories she'd tell in a whisper about
children growing up and getting themselves free.
And the children leaned in.
And listened real hard.

And in the daytime when there was some
few minutes for a slave to rest a bit,
Big Mama taught Soonie's great-grandma to sew
colored thread into stars and moons and roads

that slave children grew up and followed
late in the night, a piece of quilt and
the true moon leading them.

Years passed.

Big Mama moved on
to the next world.

And Soonie's
great-grandma grew up,
jumped broom with a
young man named Ensler.

Had herself a baby girl and
named that child Mathis May.
Loved that baby up so.
Yes, she loved that baby up.

And one day Mathis May
would be Soonie's grandma,
but not for a long,
long time yet.

In the meantime,
she learned to sew.
Beautiful girl-child
learned to sew.

WHEN MATHIS MAY WAS SEVEN,
she got sold away.
Took a star from her mama's blanket,
took a little piece of the road.
Pressed it to her face when she
wanted to remember back home.
Held it to her heart to feel back home.
Got herself a piece of muslin
and some thread somewhere
and kept up her sewing.
Sewed so fine, she was making clothes
for everyone in the big house
and slaves too.

FOR SALE,
THE THREE FOLLOWING
SLAVES,
HANNIBAL, about 30 Years old, an excellent House Servant, of Good Character.
WILLIAM, about 35 Years old, a Labourer.
NANCY, an excellent House Servant and Nurse.
TO BE LET,
MALE and FEMALE
SLAVES,
ROBERT BAGLEY
WILLIAM BAGLEY
JOHN ARMS
JACK ANTONIA
PHILIP
HARRY
LUCY
ELIZA
CLARA
FANNY
SARAH
Also for Sale, at
Fine Rice, Gram,
Needles, Pins,
CASH!
persons that have SLAVES to dispose of, will do well by giving me a call, as I will give the
HIGHEST PRICE FOR
Men, Women, &
CHILDREN.

And at night, she sewed stars
and moons and roads—
tiny patch pieces of stars
and moons and roads.

Slaves whispered what no one was allowed to say:
That Mathis know how to make . . .

. . . a Show Way.

Came to her when they needed to talk;
came to her for the stories of brave people;
came to her for the patch pieces
just before they disappeared into the night.

But Mathis May stayed on, grew tall and straight-boned,

jumped broom with another slave.

That slave was killed
running off to the north side
of the war months before he
got to meet his baby, a girl-child
who was born free that same year,

1863.

History went and lost her name. . . .

Years later—Soonie came.

Soonie's mama held her
up in the moonlit night.
Showed her the stars,
the moon, whispered
into her ear,
There's a road, girl.
There's a road.

Loved that Soonie up so.
Yes, she loved that
Soonie up.

Soonie and her mama stayed on the land
they'd always known, picking cotton
for a little pay and a piece of that ground to farm.
Called that land *Home*.
Stayed on with other people—none of them slaves anymore.
Hard work making a life—from pink day to
blue-black night—but it was a free life just the same.
And when the day was finally over, wasn't hard to find
a thing or two to smile about.

At night, they cut and sewed.
Strange lines and odd designs.
People said about Soonie,
That child could find some beauty
in so many things.

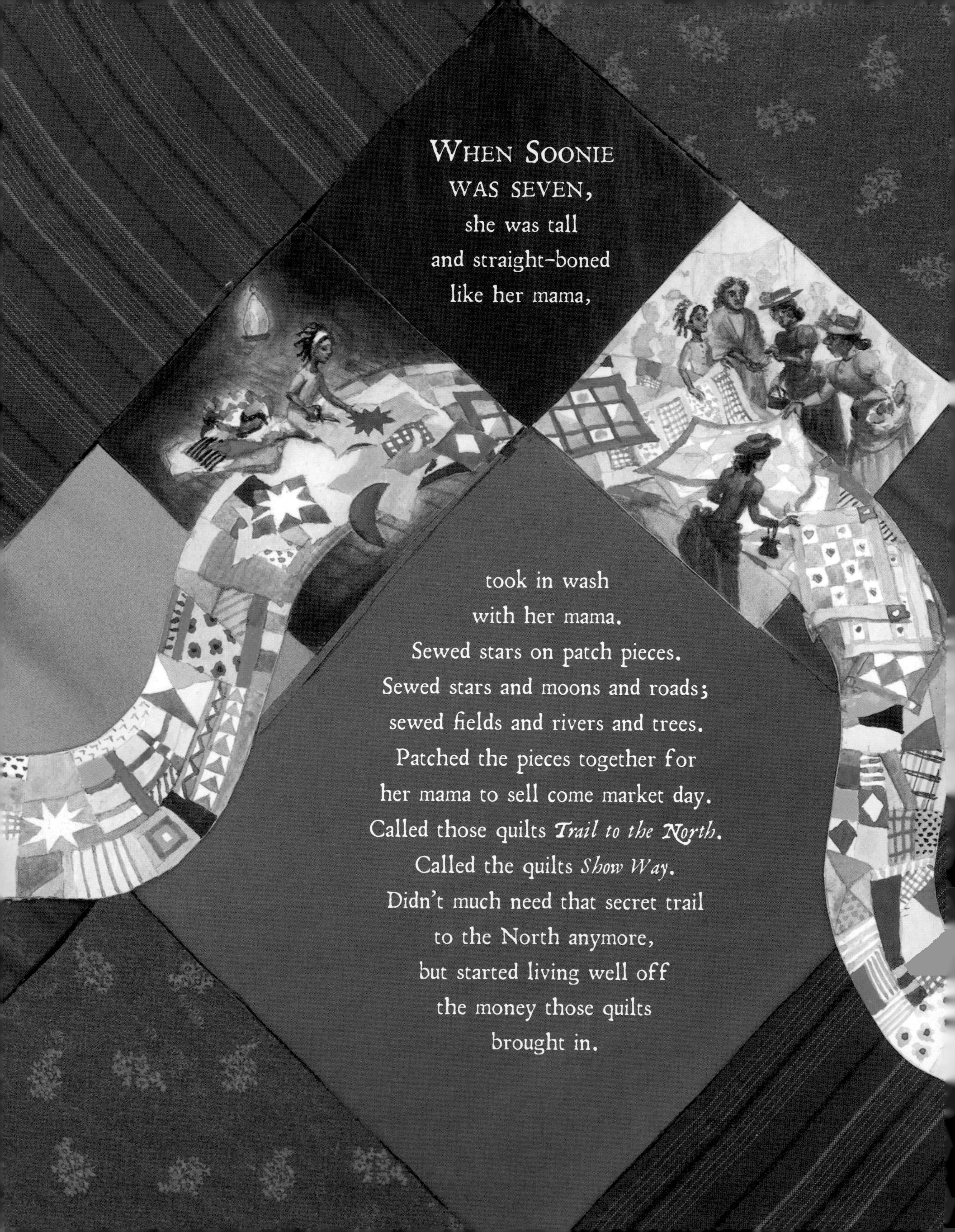

WHEN SOONIE
WAS SEVEN,
she was tall
and straight-boned
like her mama,

took in wash
with her mama.
Sewed stars on patch pieces.
Sewed stars and moons and roads;
sewed fields and rivers and trees.
Patched the pieces together for
her mama to sell come market day.
Called those quilts *Trail to the North*.
Called the quilts *Show Way*.
Didn't much need that secret trail
to the North anymore,
but started living well off
the money those quilts
brought in.

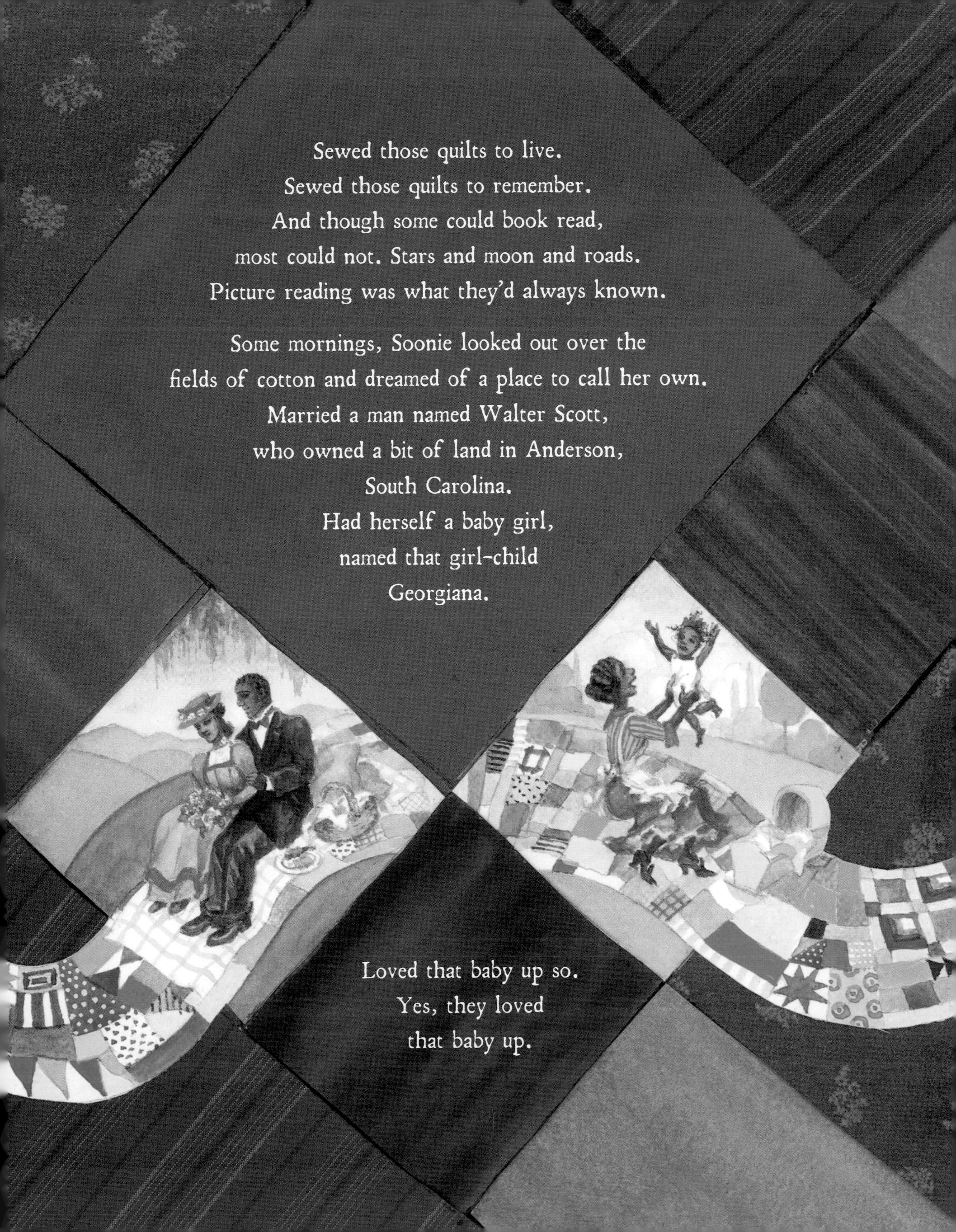

Sewed those quilts to live.
Sewed those quilts to remember.
And though some could book read,
most could not. Stars and moon and roads.
Picture reading was what they'd always known.

Some mornings, Soonie looked out over the
fields of cotton and dreamed of a place to call her own.
Married a man named Walter Scott,
who owned a bit of land in Anderson,
South Carolina.
Had herself a baby girl,
named that girl-child
Georgiana.

Loved that baby up so.
Yes, they loved
that baby up.

Georgiana, who grew tall
and straight-boned and free,
picking out words from
her mama's Bible by three.

Reading by
oil-lamp light at age five.
People say about Georgiana,
She always had
a book in her hand.
Grew up to teach at a
small school in Anderson.

Had herself two girls at once,
named them Caroline
and Ann.

Loved those babies up so.
Yes, they loved
those babies up.

And Caroline and Ann grew up tall and straight-boned.
TURNED SEVEN
walking in a line to change the laws
that kept black people and white people living separate.

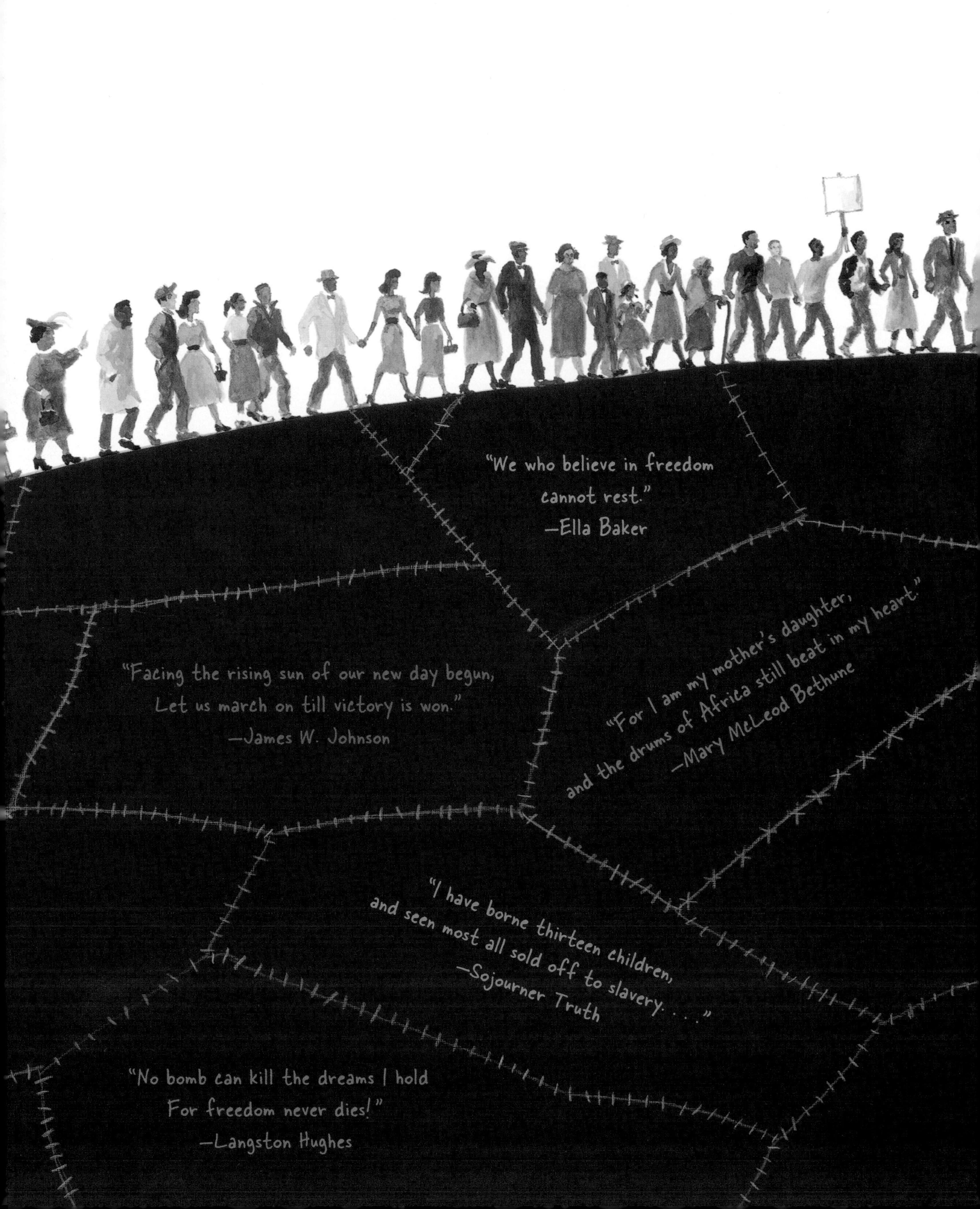
"We who believe in freedom
cannot rest."
—Ella Baker
"Facing the rising sun of our new day begun,
Let us march on till victory is won."
—James W. Johnson
"For I am my mother's daughter,
and the drums of Africa still beat in my heart."
—Mary McLeod Bethune
"I have borne thirteen children,
and seen most all sold off to slavery. . . ."
—Sojourner Truth
"No bomb can kill the dreams I hold
For freedom never dies!"
—Langston Hughes

They were a little bit scared sometimes, but pinned inside their dresses were Show Way patches Grandma Soonie had given them. And something about those patches made "Scared" hang his mean old head and walk away.

WE
SHALL
OVERCOME
New York Times.
LATE CITY EDITION
HIGH COURT BANS SCHOOL SEGREGATION;
9-TO-0 DECISION GRANTS TIME TO COMPLY
Eisenhower Bars Report
1896 RULING UPSET
DIXIE
IMPERIAL
LAUNDRY CO.
WE WASH FOR
WHITE PEOPLE ONLY
DEATH
TO ALL
RACE MIXERS!
Keep White Public Schoo
WHITE
BY
Massive Armed Force!

Ann grew up writing poems.
And sometimes she made the poems into songs.
Caroline stitched those songs into art
that people bought to hang up on their walls.

Ann had me.
And Mama loved
this baby up so.
Yes, she loved
this baby up.

AND WHEN I WAS SEVEN,
I didn't have to work in a field
or walk in any Freedom lines.
But I still read like Georgiana and wrote like Ann,
and when the words were slow in coming,
I sewed stars and moons and roads
into quilts and curtains and clothes because Mama said,
All the stuff that happened before you were born
is your own kind of Show Way.

There's a road, girl, my mama said. *There's a road.*

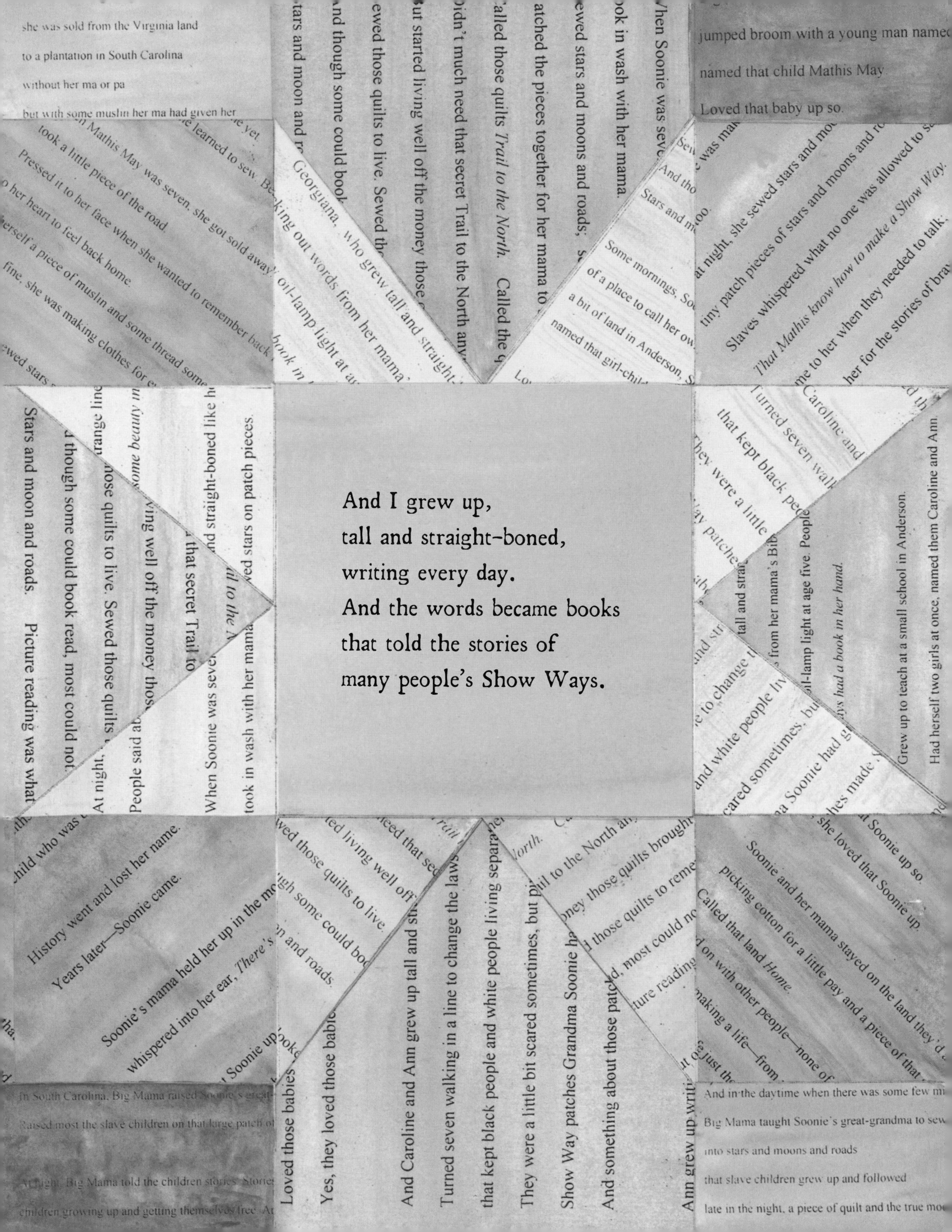

And I grew up,
tall and straight-boned,
writing every day.
And the words became books
that told the stories of
many people's Show Ways.

Georgiana, who grew tall and s
picking out words from her ma
Ann grew up tall and st
even walking in a line to change
kept black people and white people
They were a little bit scared sometimes, bu
Grandma Soonie had g
about those patches made
to a plantation in South C
without her ma or pa
with some muslin he
needles she got
History went and lost her name.
Years later—Soonie came.
Soonie's mama h
whispered
In the n
When Mathis May wa
took a little piece of the road.
Pressed it to her face when she wante
Reading by oil-lamp light at age
She always had a book in her hand.
Grew up to teach at a small school in Anders
All the stuff that happened before you were born is your own kind
Loved that baby up so.
Yes, they loved that baby up.
Soonie and her mama st
picking cotton for a little
Called that land Home.
Stayed on with other peop
Hard work making a l
but it was a free
wasn't hard
there was some few minutes for a slave to re
Grandma to sew colored thread
nd in the daytime when there was
g Mama taught Soonie's great-gra
to stars and moons and roads
at slave children grew up and follo

Had a baby and named that child
Toshi Georgiana.

Loved that Toshi up so.
Yes, I loved that Toshi up.

So some mornings, I start all over.
Holding tight to little Toshi,
I whisper a story that came before her . . .

Now, Soonie was your great-great-grandma.
And when Soonie's great-grandma was seven . . .

TOSHI GEORGIANA
JACQUELINE
CAROLINE
ANN

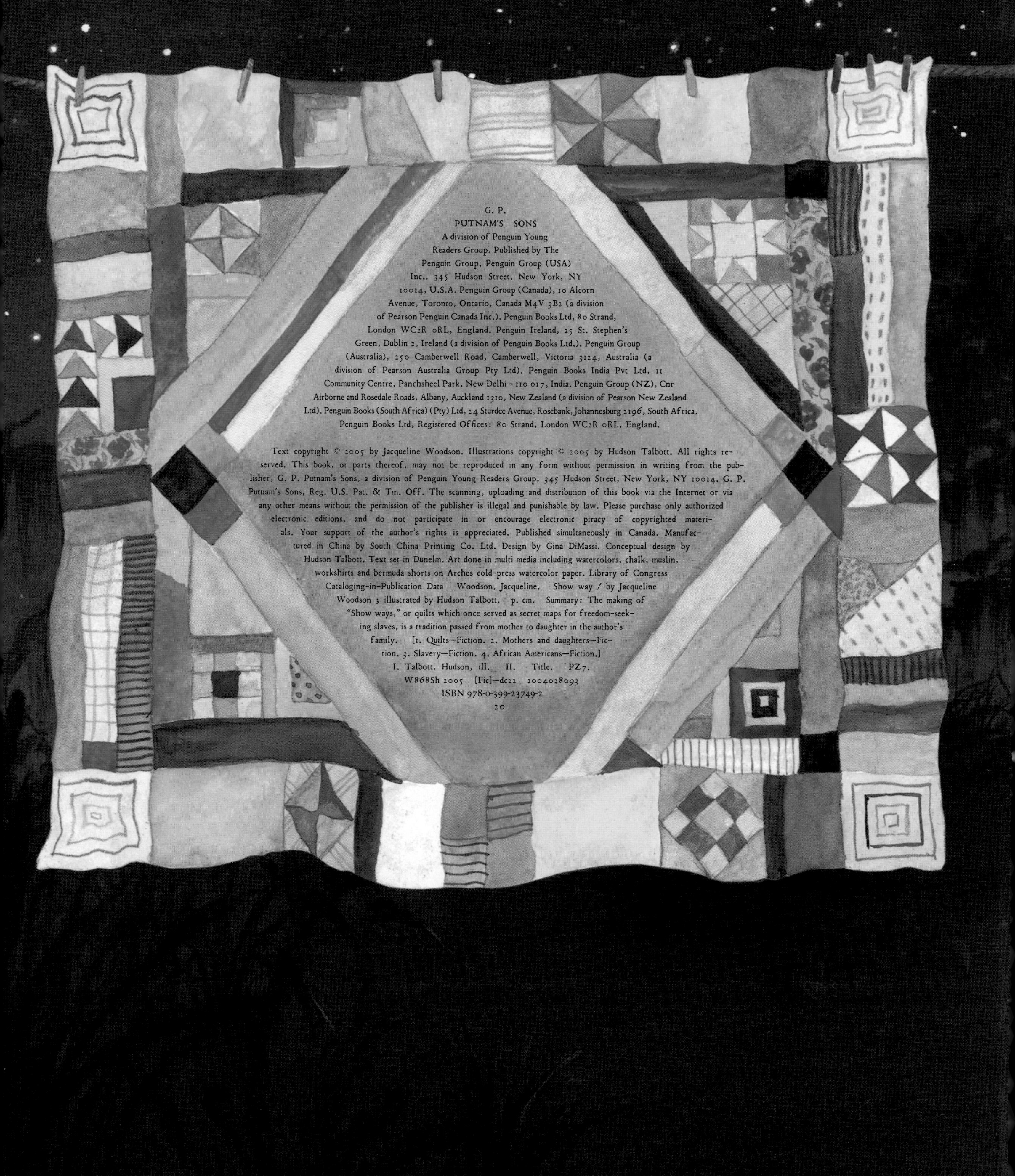

G. P.
PUTNAM'S SONS
A division of Penguin Young
Readers Group. Published by The
Penguin Group. Penguin Group (USA)
Inc., 345 Hudson Street, New York, NY
10014, U.S.A. Penguin Group (Canada), 10 Alcorn
Avenue, Toronto, Ontario, Canada M4V 3B2 (a division
of Pearson Penguin Canada Inc.). Penguin Books Ltd, 80 Strand,
London WC2R 0RL, England. Penguin Ireland, 25 St. Stephen's
Green, Dublin 2, Ireland (a division of Penguin Books Ltd.). Penguin Group
(Australia), 250 Camberwell Road, Camberwell, Victoria 3124, Australia (a
division of Pearson Australia Group Pty Ltd). Penguin Books India Pvt Ltd, 11
Community Centre, Panchsheel Park, New Delhi - 110 017, India. Penguin Group (NZ), Cnr
Airborne and Rosedale Roads, Albany, Auckland 1310, New Zealand (a division of Pearson New Zealand
Ltd). Penguin Books (South Africa) (Pty) Ltd, 24 Sturdee Avenue, Rosebank, Johannesburg 2196, South Africa.
Penguin Books Ltd, Registered Offices: 80 Strand, London WC2R 0RL, England.

 Published simultaneously in Canada. Manufactured in China by South China Printing Co. Ltd. Design by Gina DiMassi. Conceptual design by Hudson Talbott. Text set in Dunelm. Art done in multi media including watercolors, chalk, muslin, workshirts and bermuda shorts on Arches cold-press watercolor paper. Library of Congress Cataloging-in-Publication Data Woodson, Jacqueline. Show way / by Jacqueline Woodson ; illustrated by Hudson Talbott. p. cm. Summary: The making of "Show ways," or quilts which once served as secret maps for freedom-seeking slaves, is a tradition passed from mother to daughter in the author's family. [1. Quilts—Fiction. 2. Mothers and daughters—Fiction. 3. Slavery—Fiction. 4. African Americans—Fiction.] I. Talbott, Hudson, ill. II. Title. PZ7. W868Sh 2005 [Fic]—dc22 2004028093
ISBN 978-0-399-23749-2
20